monstered

Takeaways

Blue Fin, Colin Thiele

The Dog King, Paul Collins

Fries, Ken Catran

Get a Life, Krista Bell

The Grandfather Clock, Anthony Hill

The Great Ferret Race, Paul Collins

It's Time, Cassandra Klein & Karen Brooks

Jodie's Journey, Colin Thiele

The Keeper, Rosanne Hawke

Landslide, Colin Thiele

The Lyrebird's Tail, Susan Robinson

Monstered, Bernie Monagle

Mystery at Devon House, Cory Daniells

Ned's Kang-u-roo, Vashti Farrer

NIPS XI, Ruth Starke

Not Raining Today, Wendy Catran

Pannikin and Pinta & *River Murray Mary*, Colin Thiele

Read My Mind!, Krista Bell

The Rescue of Princess Athena, Kathryn England

Saving Saddler's Crossing, Ruth Starke

The Sea Caves, Colin Thiele

Seashores and Shadows, Colin Thiele

Space Games, Mike Carter

Spy Babies, Ian Bone

Timmy, Colin Thiele

Twice Upon a Time, John Pinkney

Wendy's Whale, Colin Thiele

The Worst Year of My Life, Katherine Goode

monstered

BERNIE MONAGLE

Lothian
BOOKS

Thomas C. Lothian Pty Ltd
11 Munro Street, Port Melbourne, Victoria 3207
www.lothian.com.au

Author's website: www.berniemonagle.com

Copyright © Bernie Monagle 2001
First published 2001

National Library of Australia
Cataloguing-in-publication data:

Monagle, Bernie.
Monstered.

ISBN 0 7344 0255 4.

I. Title.

A823.4

Cover design by Michelle Mackintosh
Book design by Paulene Meyer
Printed in Australia by Griffin Press Pty Limited

contents

It takes a whole village to
raise a child — *African proverb*

*For the gentle men of my village,
my elders, teachers and mentors:
Fr Pat Jackson, Shelton Bond,
Tony Redmond, Terry Monagle.*

1
waiting

Pᴀᴛ ᴄʀᴏᴜᴄʜᴇᴅ ʙᴇʜɪɴᴅ the top wall of the bell tower and squinted across the valley to the huge cypress tree on the road to the reservoir. He watched intently for Minnie to wave the green flag that would signal that the target was in sight. It would signal too that the time had come for him to do his part. It would mean that the plan was on track and just might work. It just might also mean that Bugge and Kosta would get theirs.

He briefly glanced around him at the view then quickly dragged his eyes back to watch the tree house in the cypress. He could see all of Emberton, most of the valley and the roads that led beyond the circle of hills. The bell tower was unusual; the other churches he could see all had pointy spires while his tower was flat like a castle piece in chess. His church was situated on the biggest hill and so Pat, perched on its blunt bell loft, was the highest thing in the town. He'd squeezed through the iron-grille gate and climbed up here for the first time only a week ago. It was the same day he'd met the brown-eyed girl on that stormy trip to Melbourne. That kiss — he wondered if it had really happened; he touched the bracelet on his wrist to check. That trip, that kiss had changed him. The day before, he'd felt depressed and helpless. A storm had ripped through in the morning and he'd got off the train that afternoon believing anything was possible. He'd had the guts to sneak into the church and climb the ladder past the bells. He'd even given Bugge and Kosta the one-finger salute that day and then suffered the consequences.

It was less than a month ago, then, that he'd walked past the church on his way home from school and daydreamed about a war against the Gronks; now here he was in the middle of it. What was keeping them? he wondered. Why was it taking so long? Had something gone wrong? He eased his cramped position without taking his eyes off the distant tree and let his mind wander back to that trip home from school.

But when did it really start? When was the first time he'd been monstered? When had Bugge and Kosta really started picking on him again?

2
heroes and villains

Bugge blinked through the smoke from
the cigarette end clamped between his teeth.
'Ahh, Rat Boy! Our little Emberton College
Student, don't he look nice in his uniform?'
He gave Pat another shove.

'Let me have his school bag and we'll see if we can help with his homework.' Kosta pushed Pat back towards Bugge and threw the bag to the grinning Bugge.

'Has he got any food?' Kosta wanted to know.

'Just an apple. Here, catch! And … a letter to his Old Slag from the school. I think we better find out what young Pat has been up to. Have you been a naughty Rat Boy?' Bugge was smiling, his smile far more menacing than his frown. Pat struggled to say something but Kosta, devouring the apple, was holding him by one twisted arm. He pulled it up Pat's back so only a squawk of pain came out.

When Pat realised who had dragged him down the lane there was a familiar turn of the stomach. Bugge and Kosta had left school at the end of last year so it was only a couple of months since he had been bullied regularly. It was less than two years since they had first flushed his head down the toilet during the first week of year seven. Pat had felt powerless to do anything about it and had hoped it would be just an initiation thing, but when they threw him in the river a couple of weeks later during the school cross-country, it seemed they had adopted him. They were going to get as much enter-tainment as possible out of the kid that they'd christened the Rat Boy.

'Oh dear, it seems Mummy isn't paying her bills. She needs to go and talk to the school. Now you'd think a sheila that spends that much on booze would pay her bills.' Bugge was watching for Pat's reaction. It was true his mum drank too much — most of the town knew it but no one said it to Pat. Now he was squirming, heedless of the pain in his arm; he wanted to kill these guys. He'd never cared enough about himself to resist these bullies but no one said stuff like this about his mum. He just wanted to smash that smile.

'Let him go, Kosta. Let him have a go. He won't do anything,' and Bugge was right. Pat stepped towards Bugge and said not to say stuff like that about his mum, the words sounding hollow even to himself. Bugge only taunted him more; he took the cigarette butt between thumb and index finger and fired it expertly at Pat's chest. Pat made frantic moves to brush it away. Bugge threw the school bag at him and told him to piss off. Instead, Pat swung the bag at Bugge, catching him on the shoulder. It was what Bugge had been waiting for.

'Why, you little scrote!' Bugge spat, then proceeded to swipe Pat across the right side of the head with his big, grease-grimed paw. Just as Pat regained his balance Bugge's other hand shot out and slapped his left ear.

As Pat shied away he received a slap to the back of the head. With his ears ringing and his head spinning, Pat retreated down the lane under several more numbing belts before he staggered off towards home. He was followed by the mocking hoots of Bugge and Kosta. Pat realised that he was crying — bitter, stinging tears that made him even more upset. It wasn't the pain, it was the humiliation. He was crying because it was so unfair and he was so flipping angry.

Pat had been in another world as he walked home; Pat was always in another world. His mother and his teachers said, had always said, 'He's away with the pixies'. This afternoon he'd missed the school bus. He'd gone looking for his school jumper; he'd thought it was down the oval but it was in his bag with the letter for his mum.

Whenever he walked past the blue-stone church on the hill, he looked up at the tower and the blind windows of the bell loft and dreamt about a siege. The church stood proud among the weary conifers that crowded the yellow-grassed churchyard. It was the highest point in Emberton town. The church always fired up his imagination. He and his comrades in arms were protecting the keep from the invading Gronk army. The short, crude, hairy Gronks outnumbered them a hundred to one, yet the alliance would hold the fort with sword, spear and pure hearts.

Pat's body had walked past the church and down towards Bugge's Garage. Pat's mind was still battling Gronks. It was a shame that Bugge and Kosta didn't read fantasy stories — actually, they didn't read anything — so they didn't know the goodies always won.

In his mind Pat had been holding off thirty Gronks with great skill and a slender sword when the two real, short, crude, hairy creatures had grabbed him outside Toad Bugge's garage. These Gronks were Toad's not-so-little brother, Guy Bugge, and his shadow, Kosta Mankevich.

Bugge and Kosta had hauled him off the footpath and dragged him down the lane beside the garage into the cyclone wire compound at the back, where they went through his bag, rummaged through his old fears and put a new dent in his dignity.

Looking tall, feeling small. Pat had run away and he had cried. He was twelve going on thirteen. He had run away and he had cried. Anyone else would have thought him lucky to escape in one piece. Pat felt like a baby. He was not the man of the family as his mother often said. He was a little kid. These were the worst kind of tears. As he dried the tears on his sleeve before anyone came along, he vowed that he would never let it happen again. He could not let it happen again.

But Pat had vowed that it would end before and each time Bugge and Kosta came along the story was much the same. If his whole life was going to be like this, he was not sure life would be worth living. If it weren't Bugge and Kosta it would be someone else. There was a big cloud over the sun and he couldn't remember the feel of sunshine.

Even for Pat, who had always been something of a loner, the worst thing about being bullied was how alone you felt. As soon as Bugge and Kosta walked up his friends walked away, feeling sorry for Pat but really just glad it was he and not they to be humiliated in front of the crowd. Pat's friend Whisky, who was in the same year as Bugge, had offered to beat him up, but Pat knew that it would not help him; in fact it might make it worse. Whisky had tried systematically to pick a fight with Bugge but he was too smart to take Whisky on; Whisky had too much of a reputation. It was the same with teachers; they could chase the bullying underground but they could not stop it. In fact, it seemed to make it worse; there is nothing worse than a dobber. The only way to stop it was to take the power away from the bully, not to be a victim. But Pat had no idea how that might be done.

Why did they pick on some kids and not others? Physically, there were weaker kids than Pat. He was as tall as Bugge. But he was too soft, too gentle; he had never liked violent games, he had no killer instinct. He would run to the ball but give way rather than clash. That was it, he knew, he flinched every time. As long as he flinched, he would be bullied. He inwardly cursed his parents, cursed everything that had made him what he was. Maybe if his old man had hung around he could have taught him to fight or something. But it was useless. His dad had run away too. Whisky had taught him to fight but he just couldn't break someone's face. He wondered about his father as he wandered home. Nearly everyone in town said he was a good bloke, so why had he gone and what difference would it have made if he was still around?

* * *

Bugge and Kosta left school at the end of year nine. Sixty staff who had never felt safe around them, the eight hundred students who vaguely feared them and the half dozen students who received weekly beatings all sighed in collective relief. The mood of the whole school lifted. The principal looked out the window and saw year sevens playing games. That was unusual enough, but his own urge to go out and join them had been quite intoxicating.

Bugge's big brother, Toad, had taken them both on at his garage where they were put to work washing greasy parts, pumping petrol, doing minor mechanical jobs and changing tyres. They were far better suited to this than they had been to school work, but they did miss the social contact. There was no one to beat up at the garage. That was until they saw Pat walking home. Pat lived just out of town on Mumford's Lane. The garage was on the edge of town. If Pat missed the bus, as he was prone to do, he had to walk past the two bullies.

They were, in truth, short, crude, hairy creatures in blue overalls. Both were strong but Kosta was a smaller, slimmer version with a voice shrill from whingeing and eyes so beady they looked like dried currants; you kept expecting them to sink right out of sight. Bugge was larger, kind of square-shaped with curly, dirty-ginger hair and an unfortunate way of holding his pale face up as if he was waiting to be slapped. It was a credit to the teachers at Emberton College that they never did slap that face, although by the time Bugge was in year nine most were too concerned that they might end up with their tyres slashed.

Bugge had been addicted to nicotine since primary school and took great delight in firing his still-burning butts at unsuspecting kids at the bus stop or anywhere he got the chance. He was a magnificent shot. He had perfected the art of the butt flick and could get one to sail an amazing distance through the air, with incredible accuracy. He took great delight in landing the butts in open school bags and blazer pockets. A number of elderly women of Emberton had found their shopping baskets smouldering and smoking as they passed down the main street.

Bugge loved just one thing better than nicotine — his electric-blue 1969 Valiant Safari Stationwagon with the silver reflectors on the rear pillars. It lived in his brother's garage and was not yet registered. There was no point, as there were still two years before Bugge could legally drive. That didn't stop him from working on it constantly. With the help of his brother, Bugge had been collecting parts and restoring it to its former glory. The paint job was perfect, the engine tuned until it ticked silently and the imitation leopard skin seat-covers were kept spotless. Even though it was not driven on the streets the car was washed and polished, inside and out, every weekend. Whenever life sucked, Bugge would just go and sit in his electric-blue, 1969 Valiant Safari Stationwagon and smoke.

Although the car was not registered to go on the road, Bugge couldn't resist the temptation to take it out. Just as he knew not to use his fists to bully people because the bruises showed, he knew to listen in on the scanner in his brother's tow-truck for when the police were busy. Then he and Kosta would cross the bridge and go for a burn up the usually deserted Mumford's Lane.

If you asked Bugge and Kosta they would have denied being bullies; they thought that was just the way people operated. If people could get away with pushing other people around they would. Teachers did it, so did the police. It seemed to them that if you could, you did — simple as that.

The second time Pat had been thrown into the river he didn't bother swimming back to the shore until Bugge and Kosta were gone. The first time, Bugge had offered to help him onto the slippery bank, then he picked him up and threw him further out. Although most of the school hated or feared Bugge and Kosta, they laughed. It was pretty funny. Pat was one of the tallest kids in year seven but he was nearly the skinniest as well, so that when he flew through the air and tried to turn like a cat it did look comic. Then, as he paddled around waiting for Bugge and Kosta to leave, his dark wet hair fell over his face and he did indeed look like a water rat swimming about. Even Pat's friends ended up calling him Pat, the Water Rat. Bugge just called him Rat Boy.

* * *

Pat got along well with the other kids at school. He even got along with the teachers when they weren't harping at him to get organised or stop dreaming. His real friends, though, were the two kids he walked home with. They were all in different year levels but they had been travelling on the same bus and walking the length of Mumford's Lane together for seven years. It was about three and a half Ks down Mumford's Lane to Emberton Reservoir Road. Whisky, Minnie and Pat had walked home down this dusty lane since Pat started school. In seven years they had spent a long time talking and walking. The curious thing was that they had little else in common. If they hadn't lived down the same lane they would probably have remained strangers.

Pat was the youngest, just starting year eight. Whisky was starting year ten. Whisky hated English and loved maths and science. Pat used to give him all his ideas for English stories.

'It's just a load of bullshit!' Whisky would complain. 'There is no right or wrong answer.' Whisky wanted to be an engineer.

'You can see why you do the maths and if you get the answer right,' he argued. 'If you get it right, the bridge stays up.' He used to pat the bluestone railway bridge they crossed each night and morning, and often said, 'They got the maths right and the answer is still right one hundred years later. Not like English, which just depends on what mood the English teacher is in.'

Whisky's real name was John Walker but he'd been called Whisky since birth — even his folks called him Whisky. They'd known he'd get called Whisky but decided that it was a good name anyway. It was, however, the last thing they agreed on. They had been fighting ever since. Whisky mentioned their fighting, often, but passed off their screaming matches and the occasional slaps as something to laugh at. Minnie and Pat knew his moods, though, and were very careful what they said when the fighting was bad. They suspected that as a little kid he had cried a lot. Now he was a tough kick-boxer, nothing could make him cry.

Kick-boxing was Whisky's other passion besides engineering. Pat was taller than Whisky; Whisky was only 165 cm tall but he was nearly as wide at the shoulders. After thousands of push-ups on his knuckles and other exercises, Whisky was built like a tank. Pat was never going to say it, but with Whisky's hair cropped short, smallish ears, small eyes and muscular shoulders he looked a bit like a bull terrier. Pat was several centimetres taller, fine-featured, with a shock of dark hair and almost painfully skinny. They made an odd pair — the dreamer and the warrior.

The third member of the Mumford's Lane trio was Minnie McLaughlin. She was the shortest and the oldest. When she moved through a group of year sevens and eights she still looked short. Minnie often had to explain that she was named for her paternal grandmother, Minnie McLaughlin, not because she was mini or vertically challenged. Her parents, she maintained, didn't know that she would be short when they named her. 'No,' she would say patiently, 'I am not named after Minnie Mouse, either.'

Minnie was a natural leader. Even her silence could have a huge influence. She was the last child and only girl in a long line of boys, who had all left home and were all, except Brendan the traveller, doing very well at Uni or their chosen profession. Minnie was keen to do as well as the boys. Ideally she would like to do better; she was fiercely competitive.

Being the only girl she was always going to be close to her mum, and since her dad died of cancer when Minnie was in year nine, they seemed more like sisters than mother and daughter. Minnie's mum was also a driven individual. She was a pharmacist and put in long hours as head of the pharmacy in the regional hospital. If Pat was the dreamer and Whisky the warrior, then Minnie was the mother — but, like so many mothers, she was also the general. She usually stayed silent when Whisky threatened Pat and Pat insulted Whisky, but she quietened their excesses. Minnie had the ability to be reasonable. She knew them both so well that she could get away with saying anything. She kept dragging Pat back to earth from his fantastic daydreams. She tempered Whisky's fire and insisted he not take his anger out on them.

They were an odd team of three but when they thought about it, the walk to and from the bus, as boring as it could be, was often the most relaxed time of their day.

Over the years they had invented a whole range of games to keep themselves amused. Recently Whisky had taken to playing Sumo. He'd draw a circle in the dusty road surface and one had to push the other out of the circle. He had to beg Pat to take part as he was outmatched. Whisky generally walked up to him, picked him up and walked out of the ring. The best bout was when Minnie had reluctantly taken Whisky on. She had run around him three times, then shouted at him. He fell over and put a hand out of the circle, Minnie had won and Pat and Minnie were not going to let him forget about it. They skipped off down the road chanting 'Sumo, Sumo'.

Road Soccer was their standard game. Each had a standard rock called a socca rock. It was their standard game because at least at this they were evenly matched. Whisky's greater strength often drove his socca rock deep into the roadside ditch from where he would take as many as ten kicks to get back on the road. The game would start at the bridge and they would kick their own rock along the road as if they were playing golf; the fewest kicks to the main road won. Each carried their socca rock in their school bag and although they occasionally found better, rounder rocks they had kept the same rocks for years.

Minnie's socca rock was six years old and a survivor of the Road Soccer she had played with her brothers. Her rock was called Banish. No one was sure why but, according to Minnie's brothers, Banish was what Minnie had called her invisible friend when she was a toddler. She maintained that with all the boys in the house Banish was the only one that would play Barbies with her. Whisky carried two socca rocks, one called Jackie Chan and one Chi. Pat carried Pride

Rock. Stone of Destiny had disappeared when a quarry truck had interrupted their game. The team of three hunted for the Stone of Destiny but concluded that it had either flicked up into the bottom of the truck or had been driven into the surface of the unmade road.

* * *

Pat had a few remarkable skills; he was able to stir Whisky Walker and not get bashed. Whisky was always waving a big fist in his face suggesting he prepare to meet his honourable ancestors. Whisky never hit Pat in anger. In fact, Whisky was always trying to train Pat the Pathetic so that he could protect himself. Pat could also kick an odd-shaped rock down a section of unmade road and avoid the culvert and rank grasses of the roadside.

Pat's other skill was that he had managed to stay totally independent. Although the team of three from Mumford's Lane seemed close, Pat never needed anyone. Minnie and Whisky were good friends but he would never admit that they were important to him, would never ask for help.

When Minnie's dad died the boys attended the funeral and walked solemnly with her each day and finally got her playing Road Soccer again. When her last brother moved out Pat and Whisky had become her brothers and although nothing was ever said it was assumed that if Minnie ever needed them they were there.

When Whisky's anger with his parents threatened to overwhelm him Pat and Minnie had behaved like parents, telling him not to worry, not to let their fighting get him into trouble. When Whisky got into regular fights at school it was Pat and Minnie who talked to the teachers. Whisky was always asking the other two what they thought.

Pat, on the other hand, had never let Minnie and Whisky get too involved with his life; he had to cope alone. Pat had always been a target for bullies, even at primary school. The whole time Bugge and Kosta had been hounding Pat, Whisky had been begging to go and bash them for him. Pat had always refused. He was going to fight his own battles. Minnie and Whisky respected his privacy; they knew it had something to do with his dad.

Pat's dad had shot through when Pat was a little tacker. If his mum wasn't drinking heavily before his dad left, she started soon after. Pat had been looking after himself since primary school. Minnie and Whisky had both witnessed teachers grilling Pat about his parents and why he didn't have excursion money or why he hadn't been kept home when he was sick. Pat just kept making up elaborate excuses that didn't let on that effectively he was looking after himself. Pat had been known to walk out the school gates, into the bar of Keating's Hotel, silently take money from his mother's purse and then head back to school.

Pat's dad had worked for Social Services and spent most of his time looking after the intellectually and physically disabled. His work also brought him into contact with the lost souls and odd bods that made up part of the country town. Pat senior worked for Tandarra, the care body that supported people with intellectual disabilities, mainly, to live in the community. He was often seen leading his happy gaggle of clients through town from the centre to the shop they ran. He also spent a fair bit of time at Emberton Lodge. He would often turn up and play a hand of five hundred with the mostly male occupants of the supervised boarding house.

Things might have been simpler if his dad had been a loser, but he was a hero round the town; he was a good bloke and a good cricketer. Pat had gone to cricket training once only. They had used a hard ball and he found he was just plain frightened of it whizzing towards him. Pat couldn't walk down the street without people yelling out to 'young Pat'. People round the town knew that Pat senior had shot through and that young Pat was in the dubious care of his mum. Pat had found it embarrassing at first, especially when other kids were around, but these characters became his friends. Pat guessed from his mother's disapproval when she saw him with the Tandarra clients that she might have been embarrassed by Pat senior too. Pat didn't care; these characters were great people and a link with his dad.

People like Da-Da, who was always dressed in shorts and thongs even in the chilliest Emberton winter. His walk was the strangest thing. He walked the way children do in their first pair of thongs, dragging his feet along the ground, his toes gripping tight to the front of the soles. Although walking seemed such an effort for him he was always tottering around the street or drinking coffee in the Paragon Café, with a huge coffee scroll; they saved the biggest one for Da-Da. Pat would stick his head in the door and say 'How's the scruffy mole?' Da-Da would smile and give it a moment's thought, give a thumbs up, down, or a so-so signal with his puppet-stiff arms. He didn't talk much, as he seemed to find talking harder than he did walking. When he did try to talk all that came out was 'Da-Da'. When

Pat's companions would ask what was wrong with him, Pat would say, 'Nothing good coffee and a scruffy mole can't fix.' It was the answer his father had given him when he had asked the same question.

The nice thing about all these characters around town like Da-Da, Toby and his bike, and the Kissane twins was that they would remind Pat about his father.

This was occasionally painful, as it had been when he had won the short story competition at school and no one had turned up at the awards night. But these people kept his father alive. His daydream as he walked around town was that his father was walking beside him and that when the people said hello to him they were greeting old Pat and young Pat.

'Da-da, da how's ya dad?' Da-Da would ask.

Sometimes Pat would answer, 'He left

nine years ago, Eric.' But sometimes he would humour the old guy. 'He's fine, Eric, couldn't be better.'

* * *

If Pat had gone looking for support to help tackle Bugge and Kosta he would have found a whole community. He knew he would have to tackle Bugge and Kosta. He would have to. When it was a question of physical bullying Pat could ignore it, try and stay clear and simply escape into his imagination. But Bugge and Kosta had brought his mum into it and he knew Bugge and Kosta; they would use every weapon they had.

When one of the kids from school came up and asked if he was leaving school because his mum couldn't pay the fees, Pat knew he had to force Bugge and Kosta to back off. He had to find something that they cared about enough to make them leave him alone. Pat set about finding as much information about them as possible.

* * *

Everyone had a story about Bugge and Kosta. Their old teacher said that even in kindergarten Bugge and Kosta had virtually mugged the other kids for their milk and fruit and they'd buried all the Care Bears and Barbies in the sandpit and denied it, despite the obvious proof of the mass grave.

Minnie told the story of how when she was in year nine or ten she had been doing clean-up duty at school. She was standing in one of the rubbish bins to squash the rubbish down when Bugge and Kosta forced a lid down over her head and rolled her down the hill. When she was released Bugge and Kosta were nowhere to be seen. They were somewhere else in the school establishing an alibi. Bugge and Kosta had been in trouble heaps of times but it was near impossible to get their parents up to the school and there was never quite enough evidence to hang them.

Everyone in town had heard about the night Mad-dog Huntly had parked his 1969 Valiant Safari Stationwagon out the back of the Criterion Hotel and had to get a lift home because he was too drunk to drive. When he came back the next morning the driver's door was missing. The only other Valiant Safari, the one that had been parked out the back of Bugge's Garage, had disappeared. It reappeared days later with a brand new paint job, inside and out, electric blue; the driver's door that had never quite closed properly now fixed. There were only two 1969 Valiant Safaris in the town but again there was no evidence. The police just shook their heads and said, 'we'll get 'em one day', but so far they hadn't.

Even Maudie, the lady who only talked to her cats, had a story about Bugge and Kosta. Maudie was one of those odd characters that Pat senior had got to know; although she hardly talked she had always given 'young Pat' a curt wave. Maudie's house was over-run with cats and one frayed-looking magpie. Despite her love of cats Maudie took it upon herself to feed the birds of the town. Each morning before the street came to life, tall Maudie, gaunt in her bib 'n' brace overalls, would leave her home with plastic bags full of bread scraps that she would distribute along the gutter of the main street. The birds were invisible until Maudie had passed and then they came from everywhere.

Maudie told the story like it was a mass murder and for her that is exactly what it seemed like. After distributing her scraps, Maudie had headed back up the main street and every few metres, where she had spread crumbs, she found dead birds. There were starlings, sparrows, thrushes, even a big blue-black crow. She began checking the contents of her shopping bags fearing she might have poisoned the birds herself, but the dead birds were only on one side of the street. She gingerly picked up a sparrow to examine it. It had a small wound. She realised it had been shot. Bugge and Kosta had hidden themselves on the shop roofs behind the brickwork facade and followed her down the street with their slug guns. Maudie, outraged and in tears, had to bury fifteen feathered victims deep enough in her back yard so the cats wouldn't dig them up.

When Maudie had fronted the two of them in the street they had pushed her aside and said they didn't know what she was talking about. She kept threatening them with the RSPCA but they just ignored her.

Maudie told everyone who would listen and branded Bugge and Kosta senselessly cruel. 'Evil,' she said, shaking her wild grey mop, 'they're just plain old-fashioned evil.'

But the incident that nearly brought Bugge and Kosta undone was when Yoda's legs got broken. Yoda was not his real name of course. It was Neil Swann. Neil was a Star Wars nut and was particularly into the intergalactic guru, Yoda. His big ears, egg-shaped head and old green dressing-gown made him the perfect Yoda. Neil's friends were happy enough to take it in turns to play the other characters. That is with the exception of Tim Payne, who refused to play Darth Vader any more after a trip to the hospital to get Neil's too small 'Darth Helmet' removed.

Neil lived not far from Mumford's Lane on Emberton Res Road. Their property boasted the biggest cypress pine tree in the area. Neil's dad was a truckie and had found a huge wooden pallet to make the floor for the best tree house in Emberton. It was alternately his Battle Star, a planet and the bridge of the *Millennium Falcon*. Yoda and company had built a cabin atop the floor and almost lived in the tree house for the summer holidays. The tree was so large that the cubby house was actually above the road and the traffic below became part of each game as enemy star fighters.

Bugge and Kosta had noticed that the floor of the cubby sported two large metal eyebolts that were once used by cranes. The cubby was only a couple of hundred metres from Mumford's Lane where Bugge and Kosta used to take the Safari for a burn when they thought the police were busy. This day the police were busy at a grass fire on the other side of town, one that some suggest Bugge and Kosta started. The Safari crept to the apron of the garage, waited, watched, slipped out onto the road across the bridge out of town, onto Mumford's Lane, down until it came to the T-intersection with Emberton Res Road, waited, watched, cruised down to the huge cypress. Kosta jumped out and scaled the rope ladder up the trunk and ran out to the cubby, ignoring Yoda's question from inside. Yoda thought it was one of his mates. By the time he got really curious Bugge had thrown up the cable with the hook, Kosta had attached it to the floor of the cubby and was on his way down the tree. Yoda said he saw someone from behind, climbing down the ladder, but then the cubby began to move. There was the sound of a car being revved, a squeal of tyres and then he was airborne.

When the Battle Star hit the road, Yoda heard his world shatter but it was really the sound of his legs snapping under the impact. Then from the crumpled ruins, in his shocked state, he heard a car speed away. Bugge and Kosta were interviewed by the cops but they had 'been at the garage all day' and even if Yoda had seen one of them clearly it was his word against theirs. Yoda rebuilt his legs over the next twelve weeks and then rebuilt his Battle Star but this time it was attached to the tree with thirty-centimetre bolts. When the new cubby was completed all the local kids were invited over to inspect it. Above the door there was a sign in large letters, 'Don't give in to hate. It leads to the Dark Side'.

* * *

Pat thought about his problem with Bugge and Kosta. The question that worried him most was how could he stop them from bad-mouthing his mum? It was difficult to know how to stop them talking to people unless he could frighten them off. He needed some hold over them but they were too careful. They were too slimy; they slipped out of everything. He had to make something stick. Bugge and Kosta knew how to cover their backsides.

Pat daydreamed about luring them somewhere isolated and keeping them there until they agreed not to cause him any more trouble. But there was no way he could trust them to keep their word and no way to make sure they wouldn't kill him as soon as he let them go. He'd also be risking getting into trouble with the cops; kidnapping was a serious crime. If only he could come up with some blackmail to shut them up. Perhaps he should follow Whisky's advice and just catch them alone and unawares and beat the stuffing out of them with a baseball bat. But Pat knew he couldn't do it and they would probably end up using the bat on him. He wasn't going to let Whisky do it for him, it was his problem. What would really frighten them?

With each passing day Pat knew people were talking about his mum; with each passing day Pat found it harder to look himself in the eye. He was a coward. Bugge and Kosta would always have it over him; he felt helpless. The best he could hope for was to shuffle around town like one of his dad's odd friends with his eyes on the footpath, never looking life in the eye again.

The scariest thing was that no matter what he did he couldn't be sure he wouldn't end up running and crying again. He vowed not to, but he lived in fear of it happening again. He dreamed about encountering Bugge and Kosta. He fantasised about walking past the garage without fear. If they came out and said anything he would jump down their throats, threaten them to shut up or else. But most of the time his dreams turned to nightmares and they said 'or else what?' and he ended up running away and crying.

He had to do something, but there was nothing he could do. It was a battle he would never win. He thought about finding a potion that would make him brave, or a magic sword that would lend him its courage. The heroes in the fantasies he read were often scared to begin with but there was usually a whole world depending on them to save it. There was usually some wizard or guide with a boon to grant, a secret power to develop. He only had a mum who drank too much and two friends that had as much trouble as he did just coping with day-to-day life.

3

the journey, the maiden and a talisman

Iт was hot, late February and the temperatures had hovered around the forties for most of the week. Pat was woken that Saturday by thunder; rain battered the tin roof. As he looked out the bathroom window he could see columns of black thundercloud ribbed by lightning lifting over the pine-darkened hills. He could smell the golden grasses release their stored sunshine as the rain bowed them, washing the dust from the world; feel the buzz of electricity lifting his hair. It was the best thing about living out of town, watching the weather roll in. Pat put on the coffee and stood at the big window to watch each little storm roll over the house. He turned back to the kitchen and realised his mum was asleep on the couch, her little black dress scrunched up to reveal dimpled thighs, the pale underside of her arms. There was a half glass of neat vodka on the coffee table. She hadn't made it to bed, at least she had made it home. Pat worried about her driving. He had come out one morning to find her sitting in the car with the engine running; she had fallen asleep before she could turn off the motor.

Pat had a chilling moment when he looked to see that there was no hose attached to the exhaust pipe, but she was just drunk.

Now as he looked at her she seemed so fragile; although the skin under her eyes was dark and there were lines at the corners of her mouth, she looked like a little girl. She would always be a little girl. She couldn't take responsibility for herself, let alone for her son. It was just as well that Pat could look after himself. But he couldn't really, he couldn't face Bugge and Kosta, just like his mum couldn't face life without his dad. He couldn't be the man of the house when he felt like a coward.

Perhaps he should drink too. He took the half glass of vodka to the window and sipped. It tasted like lightning. He swallowed the rest and waited for his breath to return. His mother stirred on the couch. He didn't want to be there when she woke.

He hated it when she felt sorry for herself, detested it. He would get out of the house before she came round. He remembered he was supposed to go to Melbourne this morning to get some school books his mother hadn't got around to ordering last December. He took forty dollars out of his mum's purse, scribbled a note, pulled on shorts, shirt and runners. He thought about a coat as he went out the back door but decided it was too warm; it would be better to get wet.

As he crossed the bridge into town, a charge of lightning surged through the saturated air. The lightning had been so close that he almost expected to burst into flame, to see his clothes smouldering, electricity leaking from him into the earth. For an instant he was the energy of the storm, it had charged him; death had exploded by his ear, but left him whole.

Banks of warm air, then cool, washed over him as he walked into town and up to the station. As he walked past Bugge's Garage a heavy shower raced over him, hiding him as he passed.

As he entered the air-conditioned carriage he was sad to leave the stormy weather outside. It matched his mood far better than the dry cool air of the train. The carriage was nearly deserted; it was too late for the commuters and too early for the real shoppers. He soon felt cold as he watched the showers settle in and the train bustled down through the dividing range. By the time the train rolled out onto the coastal flats the storm front had passed and left the sky a pale, clear blue.

As the train pulled into Clifton Station amid paddocks of thistles, Pat noticed something on the carpet of the carriage. After he'd bent down and picked it up there was pair of brown eyes staring at him.

'What have you got there?'

'It's a chain.' Pat looked up from the chain to see a short girl, with short dark hair, brown eyes, a small mouth. Her look of concentration made Pat fear that she could see everything about him. He expected her to say, 'Hello coward.'

Instead she just said, 'It's a good chain, it looks heavy.' Pat sat back down and the girl sat opposite. He figured she was probably about his age, perhaps a little older; not because she looked older, but she seemed older. She was more confident somehow. The carriage was nearly empty but she had chosen to sit near him, like she was curious. Now he looked at her properly he realised she was pretty too, not in that glamorous, magazine way, but there was something about her cheeks, the shape of her face, her neck, the steady way she held his gaze. Then came the moment when his natural shyness won and he looked away.

He was angry with himself. He should speak to this girl if he could. Just say something, he screamed at himself. He glanced at her again to find her smiling at him.

'Would you like it?' He'd not thought about it but found he was holding out the chain. It swung in the air between them. They both looked at it and each other. Pat had decided to take it back, lest it seem too much like he had asked a really personal question. You don't give gifts to strangers, he told himself. She beat him to it. Reaching for it, she had found the clasp, opened it, and turned on the edge of her seat for him to fasten it.

'Do it up,' she instructed. As Pat fumbled with the clasp he was painfully close; he held his breath so as not to breathe on her, still her scent raced through him. It took his breath like the vodka had earlier in the day and left his senses tingling like the lightning strike. Had he felt a faint charge come off the chain as he fastened it? When she turned back to him she smiled. The smile alone jolted him. The chain belonged on that elegant olive neck. She was as golden and shiny, full of life, as his mother was pale and bloated by it.

They talked furiously from Clifton to the city, breathless to catch the conversation up with the connection they had made in their first moments. Both were disappointed that she was older than him and that she actually came from Adelaide and was only over for the weekend with her father. As the train slid into Spencer Street Station she stood to leave and said, 'Come with me, won't take long.' As he followed her off the train he realised he didn't know her name; he worried in case she had said it and he had not been listening closely enough. It didn't seem like the right time to ask so he followed her down the street through the throng in the wet heat, under the now clear blue sky.

She walked fast and didn't pause to look around. She turned abruptly down into an underground car park. There were construction vehicles everywhere and building rubble. It looked like a disaster area. The girl strode to the first lift, which said floors forty-two to fifty. She didn't even glance at the Authorised Persons Only sign, she looked at Pat's hesitation and smiled. 'My dad works here, he's an architect. Come on.'

The lift lurched upwards so fast it was impossible to guess how far it had travelled. Pat looked at the girl in the shiny chrome reflection of the lift interior and found it hard to believe he had left Emberton only an hour ago. Then the light came on behind the number fifty and they stepped out into the sky. At least that's how it felt; the whole floor had been gutted so that the lift shaft was the only thing in the huge open space. The whole level was surrounded by floor-to-ceiling windows; as they walked around the lift they got a three-hundred-and-sixty-degree view of Melbourne.

'Cool!' breathed Pat.

'Cool,' the girl agreed. Then she took him by the hand and dragged him out towards the window so that they both ran towards the edge. 'Look,' she ordered. Pat stared down through the glass. Fifty floors below, the crowd they had pushed through moments before now looked like a river, the colours blending into a dizzying procession of movement. 'Look!' she insisted, and pointed again, not to the street below but to the narrow ledge right in front of them. What Pat had taken for a pile of sticks and bird droppings was in fact a nest. The fluffy part in the middle moved and he saw two chicks about the size of small pigeons. They were brown and sleek in part but still wore tufts of down.

Pat instantly found himself worried that they would fall from the nest. How could anything live in such an exposed position?

The girl was moving to leave. 'The parents go spacko if they see you.'

Pat was taking a last look when he found himself falling backwards. He had been so startled by the sudden flurry of wings that he had involuntarily flung himself away from the window; shocked by the sudden violence in front of his eyes, he'd almost fallen over backwards. The bird that had attacked him through the glass was surprisingly small, given the size of the chicks, but it had fiercely attacked the glimpse of Pat and the girl behind the thick tinted window. They laughed at their own fright and stood near the lift to watch the bird settle to feed the chicks.

'They're so ferocious,' the girl said.

'Fearless, frightened hell out of me,' Pat admitted, tasting the fear. 'What are they?'

'Peregrine falcons. They're just protecting the chicks; they care about them more than their own safety. Simple really. I suppose we call that fearless.'

As Pat followed the girl back into the lift he wondered about his own fear. For once he had beaten his fears — in the train when he spoke to her. That was the magic of her smile; he would step off the fiftieth floor if she smiled at him. At home there was nothing he cared about more than his own skin.

He took her hands and they spun and screamed and laughed as the lift plummeted towards the centre of the earth. At home there was no reason to risk his own safety, except for his mum's reputation, but it was not his fault she was a drunk, not his fault his old man had shot through. Back on the street the girl looked at Pat and grinned. 'What time train you catching home?'

'There's one at three o'clock.'

'See you then,' and she was gone.

Pat bought the books he needed and then wandered around town just waiting for three o'clock. He kept catching glimpses of himself in the shop windows. He looked younger than he felt. Back at the station he waited breathless in case he had invented her, she had never existed. But at three o'clock she came swinging along the platform, put an arm through his and they searched for the emptiest carriage and sat side by side on the train. Pat imagined sitting on the opposite seat from himself and watching his own face laugh and smile at this girl with her arm still threaded through his. He hardly recognised himself.

The trip back to Clifton was like sitting in the sun; despite the air-conditioning Pat felt warm and dopey, bathed in the company of this girl. They talked, but Pat remembered little of what they had talked about except that she again lamented the fact that he was too young and she lived in Adelaide. As the train slowed at Clifton Station he was going to ask her name when she stood in front of him, putting a finger to his lips.

'You look after yourself, 'cos you're a nice guy, hear? Here, wear this.' She undid the plaited leather thong from her wrist and tied it around Pat's wrist. She put a hand on

Pat's shoulders and kissed him. A full lingering kiss that left Pat's lips tingling. 'Bye!'

He'd been buzzing since the lightning strike, now he felt charged again; he looked at his hands expecting to see sparks shooting out his fingertips.

'Bye,' breathed Pat.

He was stunned; it had been his first real kiss. He knelt at the window as the girl flew through the unattended gate and sprinted along beside the accelerating train, her short hair pushed flat around her face. Laughing, she pulled up at the level crossing, waving, clasping the chain at her throat. Pat pushed his face to the window until he could see her no more. It occurred to him that he should have got off the train. Kept the dream going, maybe even scoring another kiss, but he was heading back to Emberton, back to the real world. He looked at the leather bracelet at his wrist, with its three silver charms. He sat back and ran the whole trip through his mind. No one would believe him; no one would believe him because he would tell no one.

4
the testing

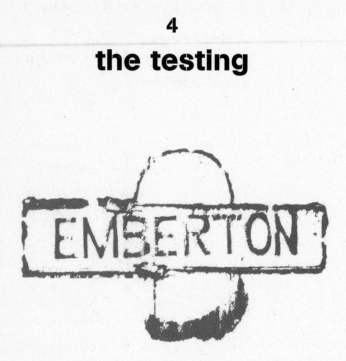

Hᴇ ᴡᴀꜱ ʜᴇᴀᴅɪɴɢ back from the station. At the church with its severe square tower he paused, looked at the stone crosses, the blind windows. He looked around again, walked up the path through the conifers.

He pushed back the heavy door and found a porch area, with a locked gate that obviously led to the bell tower. Pat looked at the gate, wrought iron set in stone, but there was a gap at the top between the spikes and the arch of stone. He climbed the gate and skinny as he was slid over the spikes and headed up the steep, cold stairs. The stairs ended at the bells, hanging heavy and silent, and the room was shuttered and dark. A ladder led to a trapdoor, which opened onto the roof, or at least the flat centre of the four stone crosses.

Pat stood at the wall and looked down over the wooded churchyard, down over the town, down to the garage at the edge of town. He felt like he had been away in another time. He had the same feeling he had when he read good fantasy. The storm, the whole trip to Melbourne, the train ride, the girl, the high-rise and the falcons —

all seemed a dream to him now. He had been to the sacred mountain, he had been enchanted by the maiden, charged by the storm. He had also, he realised, been given a talisman. He was not sure what the three charms represented or what power they might confer on him. Then he narrowed his gaze to the garage at the bottom of the hill.

Was he kidding himself, away with the pixies again? No matter what had happened or what he imagined had happened in Melbourne, he realised that when he walked past the garage these were real people. This was no fantasy where the goodies always triumph. No charm would protect him from Bugge and Kosta. What a fool he could be. Bugge and Kosta would not hesitate to beat hell out of him, talisman or no talisman; in fact they would probably call him a poofter for wearing it. He was Pat Hardiman — just an ordinary, skinny kid from Emberton, but now he felt as though there was a part of him they could not touch. Let them attack him this time, this time there would be no running and no tears. They might hurt his body but they could never reach inside him to where there was a summer storm, golden skin, a smile like vodka neat. They would never be able to understand his trip to Melbourne; they could not take this away from him. They could slag off his mum but he had something they could not touch. He had made that promise to himself before, but this time ...

* * *

As he walked towards the garage the fear still twisted at his guts but he was under control. He tried to work out how he felt different but was still unsure when he drew near the garage. He realised that he felt braver but he also felt nauseous when he realised what could happen as a result of being brave. Foolish and brave seemed like the same thing.

As he passed the garage his body made a decision; it paused on its heel and waited until someone noticed him. Kosta glanced up from the bonnet of a car he was working on and saw Pat give him a middle-finger salute then saunter away. Pat was walking slowly but his heart was racing. He didn't start relaxing until he was across the bridge and walking through the dust of Mumford's Lane. The salute had felt great but was seriously stupid. He liked the feeling of not giving in to fear, loved giving Kosta his rude finger; Bugge would have been even better, but Bugge would know. It didn't matter. He was already daydreaming about the storm, the train and those brown eyes. Pat was away with the pixies again, and only halfway home, when an electric-blue 1969 Valiant

Safari Stationwagon left the garage, crossed the bridge and headed down Mumford's Lane.

Pat had just headed over the first rise so he didn't hear the speeding car until it was upon him. He didn't have time even to jump but fell into the ditch at the side of the road. Pat was cursing himself; he wanted to throw up with fear and he wanted to cry because it looked like he'd run away again. He thought he could hear them laughing. As the blue car turned around in a driveway, Pat climbed out of the ditch, forgetting about his book parcel. He was too busy willing his legs to move, his bowels to stop churning. He walked shakily back onto the road surface and stood at the edge, amidst the swirling dust. As the car accelerated towards him, it was all Pat could do to stop his legs from collapsing. He closed his eyes, turned his back and waited to be run down.

If he could have looked he would have seen Bugge steering with one hand and brandishing a metre-long section of 50 mm black poly pipe with the other.

He thought he'd been shot in the side. He felt pressure on his left lung as his lower ribs collapsed, searing pain shot right across his back, and the back of his left arm burst into flame. He almost went to his knees but as the dust settled he regained control. Although he could hardly breathe the dust-laden air, he was not crying. He had stood his ground. Pat had a vision of brown eyes smiling, a small peregrine falcon battering at the window. He felt for the bracelet. A tiny smile now, amidst the dust, a tiny tear of triumph.

He looked down the road to see the electric-blue 1969 Valiant Safari Station-wagon, having completed its U-turn, top the rise again and stop. The black poly pipe extended from the passenger side window this time; it was Kosta's turn. Bugge's arm emerged from his window and flicked a butt at Pat. It was much too far away to carry, but its meaning was clear.

'Not this time!' muttered Pat. Next to the triumph, anger was growing, fed directly by the pain — but built too by a year of frustration.

*   *   *

Bugge and Kosta were laughing; they watched Rat Boy sink to his knees. He seemed to be searching for something. His hand closed over a stone, round and heavy. He rose to his feet again, clutching at his ribs. Despite the pain, he was really smiling now. It was the smile of the bullfighter, the parachute jumper, furiously alive. Bugge was snarling as he lit another cigarette. 'He wouldn't dare, the little prick!' He slipped the gear lever into D for drive and planted the foot.

Pat looked down at the stone. It seemed familiar, and it was. He knew the shape; it was the long-lost socca rock, Stone of Destiny. Pat smiled again, a crazy smile — 'meet your destiny, you pus-balls!' He took aim at the middle of the rapidly growing windscreen and let it rip.

* * *

When Mrs Phascolartos's doctor had looked at her florid cheeks, poor circulation, high blood pressure and family history, he had prescribed a brisk walk every day and a moderate diet. He had thought it unlikely the exercise would ever happen. Hence he was mystified when his receptionist popped her head in during evening surgery and said she had just spotted Mrs Phascolartos sprinting down Market Street.

again, it hurts too much. I think I'll walk. Try the other side, my ribs are killin'.' With an arm round Whisky's shoulder, Pat tottered up to the front door of Minnie's house.

'Excuse me, but did you order a pizza? No? What about a Mud Rat that smells of cow poo? Is your mum home?'

Minnie just stared at the two of them. 'Bring him round the back.'

'Can you ring his mum and say he's here?'

'Can you tell her I've been here all afternoon?' Pat pleaded.

Minnie just frowned and went back inside. She met them at the back door with a rubbish bag.

'Put the muddy stuff in here. There's a shower in there, you better have one, too.' She was looking at Whisky. 'What happened, Pat? I told your mum that you have been here, playing Risk.'

'Mrs Phascolartos jogging?'

'No. She was sprinting. She was wearing a floral dress, runners, and she was flying!'

Mrs Phascolartos had been walking in Mumford's Lane just on dusk when the bunyip rose from the dam at the foot of Zammit's cow paddock, groaned at her and disappeared back into the mud. She ran all the way home and never walked out of town or by the river again. 'I'd rather die of a heart attack than be eaten by a bunyip,' she maintained.

*   *   *

When Whisky made out Pat lying in the mud of Zammit's dam in the gloom of twilight he started cackling, 'What the hell do you think you're doing lying in the cow poo?' When he realised Pat could hardly move he stopped laughing and started asking what had happened. 'I'll go get your mum.' But Pat wouldn't let him go.

'No, no. Just get me home.'

'I can't carry you that far. You need to go to the bloody hospital. Pat, what happened?'

'Bugge and Kosta.'

'I'll kill 'em, I swear! As soon as we get you to hospital.'

'No, no hospital, I'll walk to Minnie's.' Minnie's was the closest house.

'Walk — not likely! You can't even stand up, and you stink.' But with that Whisky pulled Pat to his feet and let him lean over his shoulder. Then he lifted him and headed to Minnie's with tottering steps. Pat groaned through clenched teeth as Whisky lurched down the road.

'Watch m' ribs will ya, this kills my guts. How did you find me?'

'Ya mum rang, she knew you had left

the station, she must have rung t
you didn't turn up.'

'M' mum?'

'Yeah. She rang me to see i
where you were,' Whisky puffed.

'Sober was she?'

'She sounded worried. I gott
rest. For a skinny runt you're blood
This time Pat was able to stand wit
on Whisky's shoulder. Pat was stari
sunset, laughing.

'What you laughing at? Bugg
in the head?'

'Kicked me in the head, tha
have done it. Whisk, you should h
his face when I broke his windscree

'You smashed his windscreen?

'I threw a socca rock at it.'

'You smashed the window of
You're lucky you're alive, man!'

'You call this living? Don't pi

'It looks like he's been playing chicken with Bugge and Kosta. I reckon they ran over him, beat him up and chucked him in the cow poo.'

'I didn't run,' smiled Pat.

'Good for you, you dickhead,' affirmed Whisky.

'Shower now,' ordered Minnie. 'I'll try and find you some clothes.'

* * *

'Look at your face!' Whisky was stepping into the shower as Pat was stepping out.

'Pat, your face!' echoed Minnie, as Pat entered the kitchen and stood there in a towel. 'Here, put these on; they're Phillip's.'

Pat walked over to the hall mirror. 'What's wrong with my face? … Nice … purple. They're gunna be worse tomorrow, Mum's gunna go ape.'

'And your back! I'll get some ice for

your face.' Minnie headed for the fridge. 'Doesn't it hurt?'

'My ribs hurt, but the rest is a bit numb, I'll probably feel it tomorrow. It didn't hurt much after the first few.'

Whisky was pulling on a shirt. 'And what does Bugge look like?'

'You know Bugge — he's short, crude and hairy.'

'I know what he looks like, but did you mess up his face?'

Pat was smiling, sheepishly shaking his head.

'When he was stomping on you did you get in one straight punch?'

'Nope.'

'One round-house kick?'

'Nothing, you know I can't fight.'

'You can, I taught you. You just won't hit anyone and that's why you get stomped on, that's why you're always getting monstered.'

'But I didn't run away.'

'No, you stayed around to get stomped on.'

Minnie had returned with the ice in a plastic bag. 'If he had fought back he'd look even worse. What happened to your back, Pat?'

'Ran into a piece of poly pipe doing a hundred Ks an hour.'

'Ouch!' howled Whisky. 'But he smashed his windscreen, Minn. I would have liked to have seen that!'

'Bugge had his car in the lane? And Pat smashed the windscreen? Was this before or after the poly pipe?' Minnie wanted the whole story.

'I was walking past the garage, I gave the middle-finger salute, up yours Bugge, they caught me at Zammit's, I was supposed to run but I didn't, then the poly pipe across the back and then I found the Stone of Destiny.'

'Stone of Destiny?' Whisky erupted.

'I put Stone of Destiny through the windscreen. They beat me up and tossed me in the crap.'

'It wasn't Stone of Destiny.'

'It was, I found it on the road.'

'You remember when we lost it and were hunting for it? Well, I piffed it into the paddock when you weren't looking. I was tired of you winning every day.'

'I'm sure it was Stone of Destiny ... You did? That was my favourite socca rock.'

'No way it was on the road unless some cow chucked it back.'

'Anyway,' interrupted Minnie, 'he's lucky they didn't kill him.'

'I didn't run, I don't care what they did, I didn't run.' Pat had refused to let his friends help before but now he was sharing his triumph.

'So they're going to get away with this?'

'What can I do?' Pat was looking at the floor, speaking almost to himself.

'Let us help,' Minnie said as she took the ice from him and rewrapped it in the tea towel.

'Try, "what can *we* do?"' Whisky suggested. Pat let the ice pack sit in his lap. 'What *can* we do?' Whisky was staring out the window into the darkness. 'I'm not sure they will go him any more. They will be bleeding over that windscreen. You really got him where he lives, Pat. It'll cost heaps to replace, if they can find a 69 Valiant.'

'Ol' Mad-dog better keep an eye on his windscreen or it'll go the same way as his door,' said Minnie.

'Maybe they'll beat me up every week for the rest of my life and still bad-mouth Mum all round town.' Pat seemed resigned.

'Is that what they have been doing? Why didn't you tell us?'

'There's nothing you could do anyway.' Pat shrugged.

'It's not just about you, Pat, it's every-one in town they rip off or push around. They've just got worse since they left school,' Minnie said.

Whisky offered his usual solution. 'Someone should beat them up, I mean really beat them up.'

'But they'll just find a way to get them back. Remember what they did to Yoda?' Minnie was frowning so hard her freckles seemed to merge. 'There has to be a way. What do they care about, what makes them vulnerable?'

'They'd sell their grannies or each other for fifty cents. They always need money for the car and petrol. Bugge's brother makes him pay for his petrol. He'll be tight for money now Pat's busted his windscreen.' Whisky laughed. 'The only thing they care about is that car.'

'The car is the way to go, but they can fix the car,' Minnie interrupted. 'We need something permanent. Something to change them. Now we got the team working on it we'll have to think this through, make some plans.'

'What am I gunna tell Mum? Oh, hell! I left my books in the ditch, too. I can't believe she rang the station.'

'Just as well she did or you would still be in the poo.'

'Tell her you fell off my horse and Billy dragged you through the dam, that will explain the bruises and the clothes,' Minnie suggested. 'I'll go back and get your books. Can you walk home or will I ring your mum?'

'Brilliant story, Minn, thanks. I'll ring her. Do you want a lift, Whisk?' Pat hobbled towards the phone, then he turned and looked at his friends. 'Thanks, guys.' He smiled.

'You don't owe us nothing,' Whisky muttered.

'You just help us shut these guys down,' Minnie instructed. Pat was still smiling.

'Sure, I'll help.' He just didn't believe it could be done but it was nice to have his friends helping out. 'Sure,' he smiled. 'Sure!' All of a sudden his bruises started to really throb.

5

riding the dragon

Minnie had a mind that was both systematic and practical; she was expected to be Emberton Secondary's first lawyer or doctor. She stopped talking; instead she stalked along the lane on the way to the bus. She jumped into her short-legged determined stride, her shoulders hunched, her freckles having a conference in the middle of her face.

It was probably habit only that saw Minnie playing Road Soccer three days after Pat had been beaten up. Her heart was not in it, the others had to keep reminding her that it was her turn. She had seemed preoccupied since the conversation about how they might stop Bugge and Kosta. Minnie just loved puzzles but this problem was more than an idle puzzle. Pat's healing but still-bruised face was a constant reminder to her of the problem. It was important that something be done soon, preferably before the memory had grown cold, but what exactly?

For the first time in the seven years since she had agreed to keep an eye on little Pat, he had asked for help. Minnie was determined that he would get the help he'd asked for. Minnie knew Pat's mother; he had been let down too often. Minnie sensed that if Pat didn't get support, the beating he had suffered would be for nothing.

Minnie was frowning down at her socca rock lying in the dust. The others were waiting for her to take her turn.

'Minnie, your turn,' growled Whisky.

'Shut up.' Minnie was staring down at her rock. She was holding out her hands to silence them, as if she was listening to something, listening to a whisper the other two couldn't hear, listening to pieces fall into position, tumblers click into their place, ball bearings drop into their slot.

'Got 'em!' she whispered. She placed a foot beside the rock and viciously swung the other leg through; the rock flew along the ground, raising the dust. 'Got 'em!' she piped over her shoulder again and booted the rock further down the road.

'Hey, it's Pat's turn.'

'Got the pusillanimous piles of parrot's poo!' Again the rock scooted off down the road. Pat and Whisky looked at each other, shook their heads, grinned and started booting their own rocks to try and keep up with the manic Minnie, who had almost disappeared over the next rise. Minnie was waiting for them when they reached the bus stop. No one had bothered to count. There was no winner. They picked up their rocks and moved to get onto the bus. Minnie was grinning at them as they filed past.

'Whisky, I've got an engineering problem for you. Pat, you have a lot of people to talk to and I've got to go and check out the police station.'

* * *

The ancient, rust-coloured Valiant with the non-matching driver's door hit the bluestone gutter, shuddered and stalled. 'Maudie! Young Pat, he needs some help.'

'Pat Hardiman?'

'I'll explain as we go.'

'We go?'

'I need your help. Remember the two who shot your birds? This is your chance to get them back.'

'Enough said. Those two, let me at 'em. I suppose you want me to get into that stinky car of yours? Well, I will not be getting into that car as long as that dog is in the back seat and what are those cans?'

Huntly grabbed his crumpled felt hat and dragged it from his head. He looked from the dog snarling through the wire grille that separated him from the front seat to the old woman and her plastic shopping bags filled with food scraps. 'He can run behind. The cans, well, two are full of water and four are full of petrol.'

'Petrol!'

'I'll explain as we go.' The dog that had been racing back and forth across the back seat, snarling and frothing, instantly fell quiet when let out and docilely followed the mud-spattered car as it lurched over the gutter and headed down the street with its two odd occupants.

Most of the townsfolk were familiar with Huntly of the mad dog and Maudie the tall cat woman who fed birds, but most would have been entirely mystified by the two together. They both lived in their own odd little worlds. Maudie was only ever seen when she left her house at six a.m., regardless of weather, to feed the birds.

Huntly ran one of the few remaining sheep farms in the area. He rarely came to town. When he did, the old Valiant was notable for the few words the driver spoke and the possessed behaviour of his dog in the back seat. It seems that some time before anyone could remember, Huntly and Maudie had been at primary school together. As they drove out of town theirs was the first of a number of unlikely alliances that would be witnessed on this fine Saturday morning. As they drove up to Mumford's Lane, Maudie asked, 'Young Pat, how is he?'

'I haven't seen much of him till the other day and he turns up with this request. He wants six petrol drums, two with water and four with petrol, offers to pay for them. I'm to leave them in plain sight just this side of the bluestone bridge on Mumford's Lane.'

'Has he heard from his dad?'

'I don't think so.'

'It was a mistake leaving that boy with that soak of a woman.'

'Maybe … I think he thought it might keep her alive.'

'What about the boy?'

'He's a good lad and looks none the worse for wear. He's never come to ask for anything before.'

'So why do you need me to help you unload a couple of drums of petrol?'

'I don't. Young Pat thought you might enjoy the show.'

'Did he now? Watch a couple of drums of petrol?'

'No, then we head for town, have a cup of tea at that new café and wait a wee while for the show.'

* * *

'Listen up for a minute, ladies! And Morris … Shirl, get ya head out of that mag for a sec.' Kevin, the best hairdresser in the area, but also the baldest, and rudest, was addressing his Saturday morning clients at Oasis Hair Design located conveniently on the corner of High and Clowes Streets. 'I reckon all of yous will still be here at twelve-twenty so I just want to warn ya … No, Morris, you will be gone by then, shut up for a sec, will ya? … We will be having an evacuation practice … fire regulations … so when I give the word I want everyone to panic, then we will all move outside … Shut ya guts, Laurel! I know you will still have your foils in but you still have to leave the shop, it doesn't matter what you look like … Everyone knows you colour your hair, Jessie … We all know you're just an old tart … yes they do, don't they, ladies? Oh, and another thing, we have to get off the footpath so we will have to stand out on the crossing … Yeeas, the crossing, Nell. You don't want the burning verandah singeing your perm, do ya?'

* * *

Kosta had been sent up the street from the garage at morning tea time to buy some buns and although he was thicker, as his mum would say, than two short planks he noticed that everywhere he went people, on spotting him, would glance at their watches. The first couple of times, he felt sure he was imagining it. So he carefully watched as he walked past the café. There was an old couple drinking tea; the man saw him, looked at his watch, said something to the woman and smiled.

He didn't like that smile. It was the same smile Bugge got before he did something really cruel. He got the same time-check and smile from the Tandarra print shop. That bald guy at the hairdresser's smiled at him and then glanced at the clock. The sheila at the posh clothes shop actually waved and smiled. It was not a friendly wave, it was more like a 'bye-bye' wave. Kosta slunk back to the garage. It felt like something was wrong, the world had somehow changed, but Kosta couldn't work out what exactly had changed and what, if any, difference it might make.

'Bugge, all these people smiled at me.' Bugge looked at his dim friend and smiled too.

'Like this? Then did they belt you across the head like this?' But Kosta skipped out of reach.

'No, they just smiled, it was really weird … and then they'd look at their watches.'

'What time is it, moron?' Bugge had put his head down and inflated the tyre he'd just mended.

'Nearly eleven, why?'

'Why, dropkick? It's Saturday, what time do the shops shut?'

'Twelve.'

'Maybe they are all waiting to go home from work or want to get their shopping done before the shops shut.'

'They looked like Sylvester.'

'What … Sylvester?' Bugge bounced the tyre into the wall and then let it roll around in ever-diminishing circles.

'The cat that eats Tweety-bird.'

'The cat that eats Tweety-bird! Kosta, repeat after me,' Bugge was looking Kosta in the eye, a big hand on each shoulder, 'I'm a dickhead.'

Kosta looked at him and said, 'OK … You're a dickhead.'

'No. You're a dickhead.'

'That's what I said, you're a dickhead.'

'Kosta, you say … I'm a dickhead.'

'I'm a dickhead.'

'Now remember that.'

'They looked like they'd swallowed the canary.'

'There's a customer. Get out there before I belt you.' Kosta ducked Bugge's hand as it swung from behind, but was caught by the big workboot to the backside that Bugge followed up with.

'The old bags at the op shop came to the window and smiled — the St Vinnie's ladies, Bugge!'

'Shut up and get out there. I'm sick of ya.'

* * *

Less than half an hour later a tall figure left Mumford's Lane. It was Tiny Tim. He carried two ten-litre petrol cans. Tiny was an ex-client of Pat's dad. He was 189 cm tall and huge; he'd won the King of the Mountain potato-sack race at the Emberton Agricultural Show three years in a row. He crossed the bridge and paused outside the garage to rest his fingers.

Kosta called from the apron of the service station. Most people thought Tiny just a bit slow. 'What you got there, Tiny?'

Tiny carried the drums over to the pump. 'Don't tell anyone, but I got two tins of petrol.'

'Where did ya get 'em, Tiny?'

'Out on Mumford's Lane, up near the Res Road. They're just sitting there.'

'Who's just sitting there?' Bugge had emerged from the interior of the garage.

'Cans of petrol, just sitting there, but you guys got lots of petrol.' Kosta looked at Bugge.

'But Toad makes him pay for the petrol he uses, takes it out of his pay — some brother.'

'Wish I had a trailer or somethin' to get the others, they're heavy.'

'What sort of petrol? How many others?' Bugge wanted to know.

'Smells like leaded petrol to me, 'bout four more tins, I reckon.'

'Just sitting there?'

'Out in the open.'

'I reckon it was probably left by Kane Constructions workin' on the by-pass. Anyway I'm off.'

'See ya, Tiny, don't drink it all at once.'

'Na, it's petrol.' Tiny walked to the next corner, turned it and poured the twenty litres of water down the drain. He then looked up at the bluestone church on top of the hill, but Pat had already seen him and was waving his red t-shirt in the air.

* * *

Up on Emberton Res Road in a Battle Star attached to the giant cypress by thirty-centimetre bolts sat a boy in a dark-green dressing-gown, meditating. At the window of the Battle Star sat Minnie with a red dress in her hand. She was waving back to Pat in the tower of the church which she could just see across the river valley in the middle of Emberton.

This was the message that all had gone well with Tiny, the bait had been laid. Minnie was pleased; part one of the bait was in place. They needed to be ready from now on. There was not much chance that Bugge and Kosta would move until Toad, Bugge's older brother, had knocked off and left the garage. He played pennant golf Saturday afternoons and usually left right on twelve, leaving the two boys to sell petrol and Roger the mechanic to work in the workshop and lock up at closing time around five-thirty. But in case they decided to move before twelve, Pat had to watch the garage so there would be enough time to warn Whisky.

Part two of the bait rolled into the garage ten minutes later. Minnie's Aunt

Glad pulled into the petrol station to get a top-up. Bugge served her. She was a fairly regular customer, and she only wanted ten bucks worth.

'Did you hear about the accident out on the highway? Truck rolled, cops reckon they gunna have to keep it closed for a couple of hours. See ya, you have a nice day now.' She smiled at Bugge and drove away.

Bugge couldn't work out what there was to smile about unless it was the fact that the cops would be out on the freeway for a couple of hours. 'Perfect,' he muttered as he lit a smoke and flicked the match at the petrol pump. What had Kosta been rabbiting on about … people smiling?

Minnie saw the red t-shirt waving for the second time. Excellent, she thought. 'Yoda, the next time he waves the red it means Toad has left the garage and we need to be ready.'

'Should I get the Incendiary Device ready?'

'Not just yet, I'll tell you when.'

'The Force awaits.'

Minnie looked at Yoda and reminded herself that it was really Neil. There had been something fragile about him since Bugge and Kosta had broken both his legs by pulling down his tree house. His friends had told Minnie that he was Yoda all the time now and that he spent hours alone in the rebuilt Battle Star meditating. He had confided to Andrew, who usually played Chewy, that the Force had grown dim, that he felt at times like the Force was not with him. The Dark Side had grown strong. Neil's parents were taking him to a shrink. Neil didn't mind; it turned out that the shrink was a Trekkie. It wasn't Star Wars but it was the next best.

Whisky was waiting under the bluestone bridge next to the railway tracks; the tough part of his job was over. It had taken him and Tiny nearly two hours to set up the bridge. The engineering problem had seemed simple; he had to be able to block the road very quickly in a way that could not be unblocked easily. It had to look like some kind of accident or Bugge and Kosta would work out that they were being set up. It was important, Minnie insisted, that Whisky not be seen. When Minnie had begun the planning she suggested putting logs across the road or staging a breakdown. Whisky knew that logs or a stalled vehicle would not stop a desperate Bugge and Kosta.

Whisky had always admired the bridge on Mumford's Lane that spanned the railway tracks. The whole thing was constructed with stone. Most people didn't appreciate Whisky's bridge because unless you were a train driver all you saw were two bluestone walls as Mumford's Lane crossed above the cutting. The two walls stopped cars from falling down onto the tracks. The walls were pretty simple. They were three courses of bluestone blocks with a capstone row of huge metre-and-a-half-long pitchers that had been trimmed so their edges formed a fancy border. Over the last couple of days Whisky had taken a cold chisel and chipped away at the cement around the two end pitchers closest to Mumford's Lane. It had cost him every fingernail and much skin; it had been hard work as each bluestone block weighed well over a hundred kilos, but using wedges and a sledge hammer he was able to free them. They still sat in place, looking as though the wall had not been tampered with.

All that had been left to do, with Tiny's help, was to stand the pitchers on end, close to the inner edge of the wall with a pinch bar protruding out above the cutting. The stones and the levers were positioned so that all Whisky had to do was lean on the pinch bar and the stone would lean inwards then flip, end over, onto the road. Whisky could then scoot under the bridge, lean on the other lever and, 'clunk', the road would be blocked and Whisky would be invisibly tucked in the gorse hedge just down the tracks. It would all be done in less than a minute and, although it didn't look much like an accident, there was no way Bugge and Kosta could be sure they were being set up by the Mumford's Lane Mob. The only downside to Whisky's plan was that he would have to winch the stones off the road afterwards; that meant he wouldn't get to see what happened next. But the group agreed that they wanted to break the law as little as possible, so the lane had to be cleared and, if possible later, the stones put back in place.

Everyone waited for Bugge's brother to leave. Kosta waited for customers and Bugge's brother to leave. Bugge's brother put his golf clubs in the boot of the Statesman. Bugge hovered around waiting for him to leave. Pat sat in the tower of the church, waiting for Bugge's brother to leave, thinking about the last month and fantasising about a girl with brown eyes. Minnie and Yoda sat in the Battle Star and waited for Bugge's brother to leave. Whisky sat on the bridge, watching the Battle Star, waiting for the signal, waiting for Bugge's brother to leave. Half the town went about their business waiting for the siren to go off, the other half of the town didn't know anything was going on.

Then Pat waved the red t-shirt for the third time; Bugge's brother had just left the garage. Minnie waved the red dress, Whisky waved his orange boardshorts — they were as close as he could find to red. Then they waited. There was no guarantee that Bugge and Kosta would do anything. The whole plan relied on them sticking their necks out. Perhaps the sight of the broken windscreen would stop them from driving the car; perhaps the memory of the last time they drove out Mumford's Lane would deter them. Perhaps they didn't want or need the petrol; maybe they had found a way to pinch petrol off Bugge's brother.

Minnie had explained to the others that it wasn't a matter of what Bugge and Kosta needed; it was an opportunity to get something for nothing, to take someone else down. It was not about greed, it was about power. Minnie had told the others that she was sure Bugge would not be able to resist the petrol, not because he needed it, but because he couldn't help himself. She said she would bet her life on it. The whole plan relied on Bugge and Kosta doing what Minnie expected them to do. If she guessed wrong at any point the whole plan would fall apart. 'But what have we got to lose?' she asked Pat and Whisky.

'All those people I asked for help will be disappointed,' Pat pointed out.

'Maybe so, but they're only doing it because you asked them, Pat.'

'I suppose so,' he conceded. In fact, the whole process had surprised him. When Minnie had outlined the plan he had felt a little sick about talking to all these people. It was an odd request and he could see no reason why they would want to go out of their way for him. He explained it to himself that it was about Bugge and Kosta; they had pissed off a lot of people and their reputation had done the rest. It seemed everyone was just looking for a way to bring them down.

But now that he thought about it, people wanted to do something for him too. It made sense for the ones who knew his mum or dad; they had known him most of his life. Those his dad had worked with had always been super friendly and had often cheered him up with their greetings. Perhaps it was just that it was a small town, after all, and they were just looking after their own. It had been one thing to let Minnie and Whisky help, but now it seemed he would owe half the town.

The thing that surprised him most was it didn't seem to matter. Really, he kind of liked it. He was not just Pat the loner, he was Pat Hardiman, part of the Mumford's Lane Mob — part of the Emberton Mob. He hadn't felt like that before, or at least not since he had walked the streets with his dad when he was a munchkin.

* * *

Kosta waited for Bugge to get the keys and ask Roger the mechanic to mind the shop for a few minutes. 'According to that bird we have about an hour and a half before the cops are back in town.' Bugge informed Kosta.

'Do we have to do this?' Kosta asked. Bugge was driving up the driveway and backing down. He did it all the time. It was usually the only way he could get to drive the car. Next he drove out onto the street and parked. They often had to juggle cars around as they finished one and had to bring in the next one to be worked on. It was not legal for Bugge and Kosta to drive on the street at all, but they had always got away with this simple business. Even when they intended to go for a burn up Mumford's Lane they still made out they were just moving the cars around. People were so used to seeing Bugge drive his car around the garage compound that they no longer took any notice.

'Yeah, we do! We gotta stick to our routine, our safety procedure. You're supposed to be looking around,' Bugge ordered.

'There's no one on the street except Tiny heading back for two more cans.'

'Where's Tiny? I can't see him.'

'He's not. I just want you to stop farting around. We could have been out there and back by now.'

'If they impound the car I won't get it back until I'm eighteen, dickhead.'

'The car's not roadworthy with this windscreen. I'm not happy.'

'What? The car's not even registered, like a few cracks in the windscreen are gunna make any difference!'

'Please yourself, but I'm not happy, Bugge. I'm not happy.'

'Kawitch ya whingeing,' growled Bugge

as he lit a cigarette and flicked the match out the window.

'They was smilin' like Sylvester,' Kosta muttered.

'Wot?'

'They woz smilin', Bugge.'

'We'll be smilin' when we don't need to pay for petrol. Now shutit. All clear?'

Kosta took a last look down the street and nodded. Bugge pulled out and headed for the bridge. Kosta sat silent now, shaking his head. He looked again at the fist-size spiral of cracks in the windscreen and traced them with his finger where they spread across the glass.

Had he kept watching out the back window as they crossed the bridge he might have seen a pair of green satin boxer shorts being waved from the tower of the church on top of the hill. If the bus-stop end of Mumford's Lane weren't in a depression he and Kosta would have seen a green nightie waving from the tree house on the Res Road and a green tea towel answering from the bridge at the other end of Mumford's Lane.

Whisky shoved the tea towel into his bag and slid down under the bridge so that he could just see the road; all he could see was a cloud of dust at the other end that had to be Bugge and Kosta.

In the Battle Star, Minnie looked at Yoda. 'It's time.'

Yoda pulled his face into the cheesy squint he thought of as an inscrutable smile and pulled on his rubber gloves. 'A liberal amount of Degabar Slime.' He smiled. Yoda was squeezing an entire cartridge of Liquid Nails onto a piece of paper. 'Smells like my home planet,' he observed.

Minnie stood the boating distress flare in the middle of it and hovered over the brown sticky mess. 'A caramel birthday cake with one candle.'

Yoda was busy trying to stop the pile from sliding away but as it started to set he was able to push the mound into a messy, very sticky, brown ball. Yoda looked up at Minnie. 'I hope they not take too long or Yoda be stuck to Yoda.'

Minnie smiled and looked at the corner where she hoped the blue Valiant would soon appear.

Pat waited in the tower unable to see anything, unable to do any more until he got the final signal. He had been daydreaming about everything that had led to this moment. Thinking about his dad. Thinking about the girl on the train. Holding on to the memory like a talisman. He spun the three charms on the bracelet again. 'Wake up,' he growled at himself. 'Stop daydreaming.' He had to be ready to really move.

When he saw that green nightie waving from the tree house for the second time he would have to grab the siren they had borrowed from the footy club and run.

* * *

'Someone has done something to the bridge, Bugge.'

'Probably someone pinchin' bluestones. Tiny said the drums were on the other side of the bridge.'

'Someone has stood two on their ends, Bugge. I'm not happy.'

'Shut up. Look, there's the petrol, just as Tiny said.'

'I'm happy.'

'You can put them in the back. I'll just drop a U-ee, so we can head straight back.'

'I'm not happy — Ouch, all right, ya don't have to hit me.' Kosta had the tailgate of the Stationwagon down and was putting the first can into the back when the earth moved. There was a dull 'Oomph' as if the earth had been kicked in the guts. Kosta turned to see the bluestone pitcher lying across the bridge. 'Bugge! Bugge ... I'm not happy!'

Bugge looked out through the windscreen and was out of the car in an instant. 'I think we can still fit through.'

As they watched, the second stone swayed, then leaned towards the bridge.

'Ahhh hell!' muttered Bugge, as the second stone thumped onto the roadside. Then he was sprinting to the bridge. He looked over one side of the bridge and then the other. He jumped over the stones and climbed down under the bridge. He found no one. He stood on the tracks, hands in the pockets of his dark-blue overalls.

'Bugge, how we gunna get the car back?'

'Let's move these stones.'

'They look heavy.'

'C'mon.' The two of them tried and failed to get their fingers under the stone. 'Try and just slide them in the dirt.'

'My feet keep slipping,' complained Kosta. 'Could we push them with the car?'

Bugge considered the problem. 'We could, but it would stove in the bumper bar.'

'Back up and push with the tow bar.'

'Yeah, we can try, you guide me.' Bugge dashed back to the car, put the last two cans in, slammed the tailgate and did a reverse of the U-ee that he had done a minute before so that he was now backing towards the bridge. Kosta was waving frantically to help him line up the end of the nearest stone.

'Slow, over, over. Stop!' Bugge felt the car meet the stone.

Whisky was back under the bridge. If they were able to move the stone he would find some way to stop them. He decided that he would have to act before they got the stone clear. He crouched and waited. He hadn't expected them to be able to shift the stone. It might not matter much that he was seen but they had to head towards the station. They could not be allowed to go back along Mumford's Lane.

Bugge started to push the stone, but as it moved it spun around, so that the far end of it bit into the rear panel of the car.

'Stop! Stop!' Kosta yelled, but it was far too late.

Bugge felt and heard the crump of the panel collapsing inward. He was swearing as he walked down the side of the car. He groaned and then began blaming Kosta.

'Why didn't ya tell me? You're supposed to guide me.' Then he started swearing again and didn't draw breath for a full minute. Tucked back in his gorse bush,

Whisky was smiling so hard that he was in real pain just trying not to laugh.

'We'll have to go through town. The cops won't be back for an hour or so.'

'Just drive through town? Cool. But won't someone see us?'

'No, stupid, we drive past the station but take the scenic drive through the gardens down by the river, sneak out Maxwell Street and into the garage. I've been tempted to do it before.'

'I'm not happy. I said I'd be home early. We gotta go to a confirmation.'

'No one will see us and if we're quick we'll be through in a couple of minutes.'

'All right but …'

'If you say, "I'm not happy" one more time I'll pull out your tongue and jam it down your throat. Now get in the car and shut up.'

'I'm …'

'Not a word! Don't say a bloody word.'

'Less than ecstatic.'

Bugge took a last look at the stones and the crumpled panel, swore viciously and then returned to the driver's seat. 'This car is starting to look like a heap ... Not a word.'

* * *

'Lighting the flare,' commented Minnie.

'Dying from smoke inhalation,' coughed Yoda.

'All yours, Yoda ... Can you see with the smoke? They're nearly here.'

'Yoda blind ...' Yoda held the brown lump in front of himself, trying to avert his eyes from the glare of the flare and the acrid smoke; the tree house was smoking from every crack. Minnie was crying and coughing as she pushed out the door. Yoda was crouching at the window. 'Yoda stuck to Yoda!'

'Just drop it, Yoda, before you asphyxi-
ate.'

'Yoda waiting, waiting, target in sights.
Bomb gone! Gloves gone! Minnie, check it
out!'

Minnie swung back through the drift-
ing smoke of the tree house to the window.
'How sick! I don't believe it, what a shot!
Perfect.' Minnie watched the blue stationwagon head up the road to town. In the
middle of the roof sat a brown plum pudding with a flare burning hotly, streaming a
thick smoke-trail up the hill and over. The
best bit was that on either side of the plum
pudding of building adhesive was a rubber
glove; it looked like someone had been
chopped off at the elbows. Minnie smiled at
Yoda.

'I just threw it down, Minn. I thought
it was stuck but the gloves just went too,
cool, yeah?'

'Cool, yeah … Pat! nearly forgot.' Minnie grabbed the green nightie and waved to Pat on the other side of the valley. There was no answer, no green boxers flapping from the church. 'Where is he?' muttered Minnie, still waving the nightie. 'If he's not at High Street on time we're stuffed.'

* * *

'What the … What was that?' Bugge asked Kosta. They had both heard the thump as they passed under the tree house. Bugge had been wondering when Yoda had taken to smoking; he had seen the smoke billowing out of the tree house as he drove under- neath. But he had decided after the broken leg incident that he'd have nothing more to do with Yoda.

Kosta looked at Bugge and shook his head. He wasn't talking. He looked behind to see a trail of smoke but he didn't open his mouth. Bugge could see by the angry pout on his face that he was not at all happy. He had warned Bugge, but he wouldn't listen, now they were heading into town and instead of sneaking through without being noticed they were trailing a plume of smoke, there were four drums of stolen petrol in the back, they were in an unregistered, unroadworthy car with an unlicensed driver. What really worried Kosta but was yet unclear to Bugge was that the whole town was smiling. There was more to come.

*   *   *

Whisky was getting ready to winch the stones to the side of the road.

Yoda took off his green dressing-gown and became Neil Swann.

Minnie was worried; what had happened to Pat? She kept waving the nightie for a few minutes, still with no sign from the church. It meant that the plan was shot, it had all been for nothing. She was miffed because the plan was ruined but she was extra broken up because of Pat. There was no point hanging around waiting. If Pat didn't get the message now it would be too late. She decided to find out what was going on. Minnie took off down the ladder, down through the paddock and down to where she would cross the river at the weir and, if she was lucky, meet Pat before it was all over.

Neil watched Minnie's short legs pumping down the hill, then he too, for the first time since his legs were broken, leapt into a reckless galloping run. He felt whole again, he felt the Force protecting him.

Pat was hiding in the belfry of the church, peering down through the shutters at the pastor and two old ladies who stood out the front of the church chatting. Pat waited. He had seen the message from

Minnie that meant the car was on the Res Road. He estimated he had less than five minutes to get to High Street. Why was he waiting? The pastor would only think he had been trespassing or vandalising his church. They didn't look like they were going to move; it would mean he would just have to run past them and take his chances. He wouldn't let this chance go by, his friends had done too much; the sweat was beading on his palms. They were moving at last, slowly, so slowly. They stopped again. 'Go round the corner,' he screamed silently.

As soon as they rounded the corner Pat was up the ladder, waving the boxer shorts and then he was off. It didn't matter that he had waved the shorts, Minnie was almost to the river. Down the ladder he went, down the stairs, over the iron gate, out of the empty church and up Paterson Street like a galloping hat rack.

He arrived at the Criterion Hotel breathless, hoping frantically that the blue car had not arrived yet. He held the footy siren in the air and timidly let out a short blast, then he grinned wildly and let out a much longer blast and stood and watched as the street came to life. The street should have been near deserted at half-past twelve Saturday morning but there were still heaps of people about. Pat was waiting at the corner of Hunter Street, just four doors down from the police station. He had one job left to do.

*   *   *

Bugge hit the anchors as they skidded towards the T-intersection at the station; the left-hand turn would take them down over the railway crossing, down into the township of Emberton. Bugge swore as he threw the Valiant into the sharp left-hand turn. He was still going way too fast. Kosta reached for his seatbelt as they hit the tracks. Bugge and Kosta head-butted the roof, the cans of petrol leapt into the air.

Kosta was out cold.

Bugge swore again. He just managed to steer the car back onto the road surface. 'That was just a bit fast,' he allowed. He was looking in the rear-view to check what had happened to the cans of petrol, when he noticed the smoke. Again he went for the anchors. 'We're on fire!' he yelled at the unconscious Kosta. 'Get out, it might explode!' No answer. Bugge ran a couple of steps towards the side of the road and then looked back. He walked back to the driver's door. 'Kosta, you OK?'

Bugge was standing beside the driver's door blinking at the flare stuck to his roof and then back at the slumped form of Kosta, unable to understand what was going on.

'Get it off.'

Kosta refused to move. Bugge was talking to himself.

'Stuff it, I'll do it myself.' Bugge opened the rear door of the car, stood on the step and reached for the mess on his roof. As he tried to lift the sticky mess clear he noticed a quarry truck heading down the hill from the station. He was parked in the middle of the road. Bugge swore again, quite filthily.

The Liquid Nails started to move, the flare was almost burnt out anyway, but as the brown lump moved it left long strands of adhesive like melted cheese trailing over the roof of the car. Bugge walked a couple of steps from the car but the strands just got longer. Bugge had to step on them to break them. Then he had the problem of getting his hands clean; he still held the smoking mess. He ran to the nearest telephone pole and used it to lever the lump off his hands, then wiped his hands ineffectually on the wood. In near panic, he muttered a steady stream of pure filth. He looked at his glue-covered hands. The quarry truck was slowing down, Bugge could feel his feet sticking to the ground as he jumped into the Valiant, covering the seat, the gear shift, the steering wheel, the floor and both the pedals with a coating of building adhesive.

Kosta was still sleeping soundly. Bugge's plan had been to sneak through town by driving around the scenic drive that took the tourists along past the picnic grounds, the swings, the slides and the gardens. The road was usually deserted and it would be only a short drive down Maxwell Street back to the garage. Maxwell Street was close enough to the garage that Bugge could maintain he was just turning the car around.

From the day he had realised he was the most powerful kid in the primary school things had pretty much gone as Bugge had expected in life; he knew the rules to the game and he played it well. But now, he drove to the turn-off for the scenic drive along the river and the road was blocked. He sat there stupidly looking at the crowd of old men, crumpled and tobacco-stained, milling about, a couple in wheelchairs and some with sticks. They were Pat's friends from Emberton Lodge but Bugge didn't know that. They were looking at Bugge, and a wild collection of old geezers they looked.

'What's taking them so long?' he asked the still-sleeping Kosta.

Then he realised they were not crossing the road but standing there to stop the car getting through. 'Get out the bloody way!' he roared at them but they just grinned at him. With difficulty he removed one hand from the wheel and leant on the horn. The men started waving their arms at him. 'Stuff ya,' he growled and eased the car forward, determined to push his way through.

One skinny man with yellow, shaky hands stepped towards the car and kicked out the left headlight. The sound of breaking glass affected Bugge like fingernails down a chalkboard. The skinny man did a little dance, chortled and headed for the other headlight. Bugge turned purple, and frothed like a winded camel. Another old man stepped out, waving a stick.

Bugge wasn't going to get through so he dragged the Valiant into reverse and headed for Clowes Street. Clowes Street was the next one along; he would still be able to avoid the centre of town. Things couldn't get worse. His beloved car was a wreck. He would have to cut back the paint to get the glue off. An original headlight would be hard to find; tracking down a windscreen had been hard enough. Now he had glue all over the interior. He just had to get the car back before the cops got back to town.

At Clowes Street Kosta woke up. Bugge was stopped, staring at the wheel, shaking his head and muttering. His hands, it seemed, were stuck to the wheel now.

Across the entrance to Clowes Street stood the staff and clients of Oasis Hair Design. They had been standing out there for some time now and their self-consciousness had faded. Some had cuts half done, one had a plastic helmet with strands sticking out. Laurel had foils in her hair, most were wearing the flamingo-patterned plastic protectors. Kevin was still trying to cut hair; he had a wedding to do in half an hour. Jessie, having grown bored with standing around on the crossing, had started teaching the others to boot scoot.

So, when he woke up, Kosta was confronted by his mother's friend, sporting a plastic helmet complete with white slime, leading a motley gang in a boot scoot across the intersection of Clowes Street.

'What a nightmare. I was supposed to be at a confirmation and I was late and when I got there all these people kept smiling at me.' Kosta focused on what was happening on the crossing in front of him. 'Bugge? What's happening? … What happened to my head? What are you doing driving down High Street? Bugge, what the hell is going on? … Bugge? I told you they were smiling at me. Bugge? Bugge? Get us out of here. Bugge!? Drive!'

'I need a smoke. Kosta, light me a smoke, my hands are stuck.' Bugge looked like he was in shock; he looked like he would either cry or explode. Kosta quickly lit a smoke and put it between Bugge's trembling lips.

'Now just get us back to the garage …
If you don't start driving I'm gunna get out
and leave you here.'

Bugge turned his baleful stare on
Kosta like a punished puppy.

'Just drive, I won't get out,' Kosta
relented; he didn't want to get out with all
these lunatics loose on the street.

Bugge shook his head and swung the
car back onto High Street, looking totally
dazed. Bugge was driving in slow motion as
if he didn't trust himself to drive at more
than fifteen Ks an hour. At the next corner,
Redmond Street, the entire Tangarra Supervised Day Care, staff and clients, were frantically waving at them.

'Even the nuffers are smiling at us,'
Kosta wailed.

Bugge pointed the car up the main
street.

'We could just drive out of town,' suggested Kosta.

The only right-hand turn off High Street was the one that led out to the freeway. Rory Doherty and all the drunks from the Criterion Hotel blocked the intersection. They were having a wonderful time. Rory was blocking one side of the traffic island; on the other, Gwen of Sadie's Fashions had her rack of specials blocking the road.

'We could just back up and head out the way we came.'

Bugge motioned his head towards his rear-view mirror. The road was filled with people following them down the road. There were people dancing in flamingo sheets, people in wheelchairs jiving around, people with glasses of beer. It was a carnival.

'Where did all these people come from?' Kosta wanted to know. It wasn't just the people blocking the turn-offs, heaps of people were hanging around outside the closed shops, some waving, others just smiling. 'There's no parade on today is there? I can smell petrol.'

'We're it.'

'There's the chicks from the St Vinnie's shop. They smiled at me this morning. Seems we're heading for Hunter Street, Bugge. You know what's down Hunter Street? The cop shop.' The three old ladies from the opportunity shop were spread across the High Street. 'We could get through, maybe.'

As Kosta spoke, Huntly in his battered Valiant pulled out of a park in front of the stock agents. He parked across the High Street, leaving Bugge no option but to turn down Hunter Street. Huntly and Maudie sat in the front seat and happily waved at the lads in the now battered 1969 electric-blue Valiant Safari Stationwagon. They could see old Maudie cackling fit to bust.

*   *   *

Pat had stood outside the Criterion Hotel and watched the blue Safari appear from the direction of the station. He noted the trail of smoke; Yoda had been on target. He worried for a while when they must have stopped in the dip in the road but then they reappeared minus the flare. He chuckled as they were turned back at the entrance to the scenic drive; it was too far away to see what really happened but the plan was still working.

'Way to go, Emberton Lodge!' He could just see people milling around outside Oasis Hair. Again he saw the car swing back onto High Street. 'Excellent! Go, Kevin and Co.'

Pat looked at all the people out on the street and began to laugh. He had spoken to quite a few people but there were hundreds on the main street. This was like a carnival. People were milling about, calling out to each other, some had joined with the boot-scooting crew of Oasis Hair and were dancing down towards Hunter Street. He could see Toby Jug and his bike doing endless circles on the middle of the road; the Kissane twins bouncing around each other like two tanks on short leads. Goofy and his dog stood blinking on the edge of the pavement. The staff of the shire offices had even come down their office steps to see what was going on and had caught the mood. Counsellor Baynton was looking wistfully at the crowd, wondering how to get as good a turn-out for the annual show parade.

There were no mythical heroes in Emberton, no famous warrior, no legendary immortal magician, no simple creatures of furry feet and pure heart — just a whole range of flawed, ordinary people. Was this the coming together of all the forces for good? No, these were just the odd bods of Emberton. The thing that made Pat shake his head was that a couple of days ago he had felt his life to be a disaster. Now he felt like a prince. He wasn't sure what it had taken to turn his life around. Was it the girl with the brown eyes? Was it his own actions? Was it his two friends and a few odd bods?

As people noticed Pat outside the Criterion Hotel they waved and smiled. Pat wasn't even sure who some of them were, some were just enjoying the party with no idea what was really going on. An elderly man looked at Pat and doffed his hat, a pair of old ducks smiled and bowed their heads over their handbags. Pat felt like a prince, but these people were not his subjects. No, they were just the goodies. They were there because they had chosen to be there. He realised that his father was there too; it was his connection to the town that had allowed this to happen. This was the gift that he had left for Pat. It had taken him all this time to realise its value. He was swamped with a surge of pride and then, in the ebb of loss, he stood helpless at the corner of Hunter and High Streets, fighting back the tears.

* * *

It was now time to get to the cop shop. He could see Rory and the St Vinnie's ladies in position. As he ran towards the cop shop he saw Minnie and Neil puffing up Hunter Street from the other direction, their shoes wet from walking over the weir wall. Minnie was looking very relieved to see him. He waved and started walking. She was stuffed. Minnie and Neil had made it from one side of the valley to the other in less than five minutes.

Pat's business at the cop shop didn't take long. Sergeant Malseed was already standing out on the verandah, he knew something was going on. Pat's last job was to make sure the cops came out to get Bugge and Kosta. He didn't really need to say anything.

When Sergeant Malseed had noticed that something was happening, that there was a buzz in the town, he had asked around, 'What's going on?' He had been told nothing. So when he saw Pat running down the street towards him he asked, 'Young Pat! Are you gunna tell me what's going on?'

'If you'd just like to stand here a minute and wait, all will become clear,' Minnie instructed him. Minnie and Neil were still panting. Pat had seen the car coming, the others had not seen it since it had sped under the tree house. Pat still stood on his toes, straining to see.

'Why are there so many people on the street?' Neil wanted to know.

'Watch,' Pat said. Then around the corner came the glue-encrusted, electric-blue 1969 Valiant Safari Stationwagon.

'Well, looky here!' breathed Sergeant Malseed. 'An unregistered vehicle and if I'm not mistaken an unlicensed driver. Yes! Young Bugge, if my eyes don't deceive me.'

'Ask them about the petrol in the back,' suggested Neil.

'Petrol in the back?' muttered the policeman. 'But why is he driving down Hunter Street?'

Sergeant Malseed looked around, but there was no sign of the three kids that had been crowding at his elbow, there was just the growing sea of people that seemed to be there simply to watch him stop this car.

'Strange days indeed.'

* * *

'Heading down Hunter Street,' Kosta commented as Bugge swung through the left-hand turn. Bugge drove, silent and resigned. 'And there is Sergeant Malseed waiting for us. We are in trouble, Bugge, big-time trouble.'

'Shut up, Kosta.' Bugge was feeling very weary.

Sergeant Malseed raised a hand to stop the car, and a cheer went up from the crowd. Bugge pulled up in front of the police sergeant.

'Nice of you guys to drop in. I've been meaning to have a chat with you. Why don't you just pull the car into the compound and we can just step inside for a chat.'

'I'm stuck,' Bugge whispered.

'What's that, young Bugge?'

'I'm stuck to the wheel.'

* * *

By the time Whisky leant his bike against the window of the Paragon Café, Pat had already had two coffee scrolls and a milk shake and appeared just as agitated as he had been for the last couple of days. Whisky needed a drink but Pat dragged all three of them out the door and down Peterson Street.

'I've got to pick up my wardrobe.'

He led them straight to the church, into the foyer where he climbed the gate. 'And I want you guys to see something,' he said, as he squeezed over the spikes and lowered himself back down onto the steps.

'I've seen all I'm gunna see, no way am I gunna fit through there,' Whisky informed Pat. Pat looked quickly from the top of the gate to the width of Whisky's shoulders.

'I just want you to see the view. Sorry.'

'I'll wait,' Whisky offered, then walked back out into the churchyard and wandered about.

It was getting on towards late afternoon. Minnie and Neil had never seen Emberton from above before. As they emerged onto the roof the sun slanted across the town, leaving long shadows from the European trees, the high-gabled roofs, the other three churches and the sea of television aerials.

'It looks like a postcard,' Minnie said. 'You wouldn't know it was the same town from here. You could be anywhere.'

'You can see where the river goes for miles.' Pat pointed. 'I looked at this for ages today.'

'You can see for ever,' Neil breathed.

'You can see my house. It's tiny.' It was Whisky. The three kids looked over the wall and saw Whisky perched in the very top of one of the conifers. 'Great view.' He chuckled at the look on the faces of his friends.

'You're a lunatic, Whisky!' accused Minnie.

'I can see what you mean, Pat. It looks

like the town is really small and all the roads lead away from it and you want to follow all of them.' Whisky looked really flushed from his climb or maybe from the view.

'But you can, you can go anywhere, you can do anything, you can be anything.' Pat was talking mainly to himself but the others were also staring at the view, gazing out into their futures. 'Even Adelaide,' he finished wistfully.

'Adelaide?' the others chorused.

* * *

At almost that exact moment, after nearly two hours of questions, Bugge stepped down the cop shop stairs. They had finally let him out for a smoke. He really needed one. It had taken an hour to get his brother in from the golf club, by which time Malseed had been able to dissolve most of the adhesive, with petrol, and free Bugge from the car. They had spilt petrol all over the driver's seat trying to get Bugge unstuck. Kosta had long gone. His parents had collected him and, as Bugge commented to him when they arrived, 'They don't look happy!'

Malseed had informed Bugge that he would have to go before a magistrate; that he would be found guilty of driving an unregistered vehicle and driving without a licence; that he would be fined five hundred dollars for each offence. He would have to leave the car until he had paid his fines and someone could bring a trailer to collect it.

There was a dune buggy locked in the compound; it had been there as long as Bugge could remember, rusting away. He'd noticed it again when he had parked beside it. His car was still there; he looked at it sitting near the horse-chestnut tree that shaded the police station. He had a strong urge to go and sit in the driver's seat. Then he remembered how trashed his pride and joy was. It would just depress him.

Toad and Sergeant Malseed joined Bugge at the bottom of the stairs; he could go home now. Bugge took a last drag of his cigarette, took a long last look at his car, flicked his butt high into the air and turned to go home.

As he took a step towards the street he heard a whispered 'whomp'. Bugge turned as Sergeant Malseed and Toad dived past him. There was a blue light flickering under his car; it wasn't until it jumped up to engulf the car that he realised it was flame. Then a balloon of orange and yellow flame pressed at the windows. The windows blew out at the same time as the roof lifted off and sailed into the next street. The roar of heat and flame knocked Bugge flat and seared off his ginger eyebrows and most of his hair.

* * *

One block away, four young people turned to see the roof of an electric-blue 1969 Valiant Safari Stationwagon fly over two streets and demolish Libby Simon's chook shed.

'Cool!' said Pat.

'Yeah!' said Whisky, nearly tumbling from his tree. 'Way cool!'

6
sharing the treasure

Neil had to go and meet his folks at his grandma's place so he had left the three friends as soon as the fire brigade had put out the fire and filled the black shell of Bugge's car with foam. They had watched from their perch above the town. Then they had waited until they were confident they wouldn't run into Bugge. He'd be in a very ugly mood, they reckoned.

'Explosive!' offered Yoda, with a smirk over his shoulder. 'May the Force …' and he was gone into the deepening shadows.

Minnie, Whisky and Pat walked in silence down the hill past the deserted garage and out onto Mumford's Lane. 'Road Soccer?' Whisky was searching the side of the road looking for a socca rock.

'Whisky, there is a small problem,' Minnie gently pointed out. 'It's too dark to see.'

Whisky placed his stone on the edge of the bitumen, squinted into the gloom and punted it down the road. He peered hard and tried to see where it landed.

'It's too dark,' he said simply.

'Funny, I thought someone just said

that,' Minnie said innocently. Whisky looked at her briefly.

'It'll have to be Sumo, then.' He grabbed Minnie, threw her over his shoulder and started running down the lane like a berserk caveman. 'Ahhhh!' he roared.

'Whiskyyeyeyeyeye!' Minnie's protest took on the rhythm of Whisky's shambling run. 'Paa-aa-aat, he-e-e-elp me-e-e-e-e!'

Pat shambled down the road after them. 'Whisky,' he called lamely. 'Put her down, she'll throw up on you.'

Whisky came to a sudden halt and put Minnie down just as Pat arrived.

'Sumo!' he bellowed, and tried to pick them both up, one over each shoulder. He managed the weight well, but Pat's long legs were flailing about in front of him and Minnie now had him in a headlock. She was trying to hold on as he broke into a danger-ously unbalanced, lurching stagger. Pat and

Minnie were screaming at him to stop, both sure that they were about to be driven into the road surface, when Whisky tripped on the socca rock he had moments before dug out of the roadside. When they bit the dust none of them were sure if they were laughing or crying.

When the three figures topped the rise just before Minnie's gate they looked like three battle-weary diggers. Whisky was favouring his ankle and his shirt had disintegrated. Pat had kneed himself in the nose and there was a dusty trail of blood on his face. His sleeve was rolled up to reveal a tender trail of gravel rash. Minnie cradled her left arm, protecting a sore shoulder.

The view they had of the western sky stopped them in their tracks. There was one huge monolith of dark cloud stretching up into the midnight-blue sky. The sun itself was gone but the horizon was edged in gold.

The orange light that washed the hills transformed the colours so the dusty threesome looked burnished gold and rust. Pat looked down at Minnie.

'I guess this is it,' she said, still staring at the skyline.

'You won't be here next year.'

'No.' She blinked up at Pat and Whisky. 'I'll probably be in Melbourne.'

'I'll be stuck with this lunatic. He'll probably kill me.'

'You'll be all right, Pat.' Minnie was telling, not asking.

'Yeah. Yeah, I'll be all right.' He believed it. Minnie smiled and turned up the gravel drive.

'Thanks, guys, it was great. I couldn't have done it without you.' Pat faltered.

'No way,' agreed Whisky.

'It was great, wasn't it?' Minnie took a step back towards them, remembering.

'Boom!' Both her hands flew into the air, she winced in pain and then her good arm sailed with a whistle and destroyed a chook shed.

The boys laughed.

'That was great.'

They nodded. She smiled, turned and walked up her drive.

'See you Monday.' Whisky yelled. Minnie waved and the boys started walking.

'You know what, Whisky?'

'Na, what?'

'I am never going to play Sumo again. You are just an accident looking for a place to happen, don't know your own strength. You're gunna kill someone.'

'You know what, mate?'

'What?'

'This was the best day. I just wish I'd seen 'em pull up outside the cop shop.'

'It was very cool.' Pat squinted into the last of the sun's rays.

'Yeah, way cool.'

'I think we're riding off into the sunset.'

'You might be riding, I'm limping off into the sunset.'